Shanti

Faber
Stories

Born in New Delhi, India, in 1961, Vikram Chandra now divides his time between Bombay and Washington D.C. His debut novel, *Red Earth and Pouring Rain*, was awarded the David Higham Prize for Fiction and the Commonwealth Writers Prize for the Best First Published Book. His collection of stories, *Love and Longing in Bombay*, was published in 1997 and won the Commonwealth Writers Prize for the Eurasia region. It was also shortlisted for the *Guardian* Fiction Prize. His most recent novel, *Sacred Games*, was published in 2007 and shortlisted for the Encore Award, and made into a Netflix Original series in 2018.

Vikram
Chandra

Shanti

Faber
Stories

ff

First published in this edition in 2019
by Faber & Faber Limited
Bloomsbury House
74–77 Great Russell Street
London WC1B 3DA
First published in *Love and Longing in Bombay* in 1997

Typeset by Faber & Faber Limited
Printed and bound by CPI Group (UK) Ltd, Croydon, CR0 4YY

A CIP record for this book
is available from the British Library

ISBN 978–0–571–35686–7

MIX
Paper from
responsible sources
FSC
www.fsc.org FSC® C020471

10 9 8 7 6 5 4 3 2 1

I hate Sunday evenings. It's that slow descent into the dusk that oppresses me, that endless end with its undertaste of death. Not so long ago, one Sunday evening, I flipped the television off and on a dozen times, walked around my room three times, sat on the floor and tried to read a thriller, switched on the television again, and the relentless chatty joyousness finally drove me out of the house. I walked aimlessly through the streets, listening to the long echoes of children's games, tormented by a nostalgia that settled lightly over me. I had not the slightest idea of what I was looking for, but only that I was suddenly aware of my age, and it seemed cruel that time should pass so gently and leave behind long swathes of unremembered years. I walked, then, along the long curve of the seawall at Haji Ali, and came along towards the white shape of the mosque floating on the waters.

Then, at the intersection, I didn't know what to do. I stood, too tired for another long journey and too restless still to go home, and I was swaying a little from side to side. Then I felt a gentle tap on my shoulder. It was Subramaniam.

"Come along," he said. "I'll give you a drink."

He was carrying a tattered *thela*, and we stopped along the way to fill it with bread, marmalade, and bottles of soda. He lived in an old, shabby building near Tardeo, and we went up four flights of stone stairs worn thin in the centre. Inside the door marked "Subramaniam" in brass letters, I bent to take off my shoes, and I could see the space was cool and large. There were those old high ceilings, and walls hung with prints. I sat in the drawing room on a heavy teak couch, on worn cushions, and wriggled my toes on the cold marble. Subramaniam came in carrying a bowl of chips.

"New brand," he said, smiling, and he put the bowl down on the table at my elbow. Then he poured me a drink. He sat in an armchair that creaked slightly, and raised his glass at me.

"Haven't seen you in a while," I said.

"Yes," he said. "Unfortunately my wife has been unwell."

2

"Sorry," I said. "I hope it's nothing serious."

He raised his shoulders in that awkward little shrug of his. "At a certain age everything is serious, and nothing is serious." He drank, and then put down his glass on the table with a crisp click. He looked keenly at me. "How is that Ayesha?"

"Yesterday, she was very bitter about a patriotic movie she saw," I said. "She is in despair about the state of the country. What are we, she said. For a cynic she despairs a lot. She's my friend, but I don't understand her, not really."

He nodded. "Listen," he said. "I want to tell you a story."

———

A train drifting across a field of yellow grass. This is what he saw first. A plume of black smoke turning slowly in the white glare. He had gone up the long slope in front of the station, across the three tracks, and then up the rise, to the ridge which had turned out to be much, much further than he had thought. When he had reached it, and gone across, he had found himself on an endless plateau, a plain dotted with scrubby bushes, an endless flatness that vanished into the sky. So he had turned around and come back. He had already forgotten what he had hoped to find on the other side of the ridge, but for two months he had looked at it curling in the distance, and finally he had taken a walk to see the other side of it. Now the sun burnt on his shoulders. Now he came back over the ridge and saw the train drifting across a field of yellow grass.

It was 1945 and he was twenty years old. His name was Shiv, and he had a twin who was dead, killed in Delhi the year before when a Hindu procession had gone the wrong way. The newspapers had regretted the continued communal violence in the city, but had reported with relief that on this day there were only six dead. One of the six was his, one body identical down to the strangely short fifth toe on the left foot. He had never known the bitterness of small statistics, but now he carried it everywhere in his mouth. He had it now, as he stumbled with aching calves, back from his walk of no purpose. The day yawned before him. He lived with his sister and her husband in a large bungalow a minute and a half's walk from the station. In the house there were a dozen novels he had read already, his B.Sc. degree framed on a wall, and two small children he could not bear to play with. He had come to live with his sister and her station-master husband after his silences had frightened his parents. His sister had loved him most, had loved him and his brother best after their birth at her eight years, and even now, grief-stricken, she found happiness and generosity enough in the safety of her home to comfort him. But the day, and life itself, stretched on forever like a bleak plain of yellow grass, and he felt himself walking, and the train drifted with its fantastic uncurling of smoke.

The train slowed imperceptibly as he walked. It must have, because he became aware that it was paused, halted at the station. But even then it moved, shimmering in the heat haze, a long red blur. Then, again, it was stirring, drifting across the yellow. He had no sense of his own movement, only of the shuffling of his feet and the sweat trickling down his back, and somehow the train was drawing away from him. Then he was at the station. He crossed the tracks and climbed onto the main platform. He went past the sign that proclaimed "Leharia" and its elevation of seven hundred and eighteen feet, past the station master's office and the second class waiting room, past the door to the ticketing office and the passengers sprawled on the green benches, and to the arched white entrance to the station. There he stopped, unsure. He looked out across the tracks and there was the slow slope and the faraway rim. He had gone to the edge of his world and come back and he didn't know what was next. The train was now a single oblong to the west. He looked down along the tracks to the west and then back to the east and the thought occurred to him suddenly that he could wait for the next train, and it was a short step off the platform onto the black rails, a drop of three feet. The train would be moving very slowly but it had a great momentum. It could not be stopped. He recognized the melodrama of the thought, and was also surprised that he had not had it before. There was a certain relief in it. It seemed now inevitable, at least as an idea, and he determined that he would wait for the next train to see what happened. That would be the three-thirty from Lucknow.

Now that there was a plan he was released from lethargy. He was suddenly full of energy and very thirsty. There was a *matka* of water in the first class waiting room. He walked now with a snap, and he waved smartly at Frankie Furtado the assistant station master, who was looking, from a barred window, after the receding smudge on the western sky with an expression that was usually taken for commendable railway concentration and proper seriousness. He was actually—Shiv knew—dreaming of Bombay, and now Frankie returned the wave with but a slow raising of the fingers of one elegant hand that rested on an iron bar. There was an entire matinee's worth of tragedy in the single motion, and Shiv smiled a little as he drank the lovely clayey water.

It was crisp and cold and the ladle made a deep belling sound as it dipped under the dark surface.

He poured the water into his mouth. It splashed over his neck and chest, and he let it fall on his face, and when he heard the laugh he choked. When he stopped coughing he turned and saw the figure by the window. At first all he could see was hands held together, the furled drapery of a grey sari from knee to ground. Then in a moment or two he could see her. She was thin, very young. She wore no ornaments, not a bangle, no earrings. The eyes were large, there was a thick plait falling over a shoulder, and now she looked down and put a hand over her mouth. Shiv put the ladle back in the *matka*, and it dropped with a rattle into the water. He backed to the door, edged through it, blushing, and then stood on the platform wiping his face.

"Who is that in there?" he asked Frankie Furtado, whose face lit up at the question. Frankie was really a movie star trapped by his railway father and railway grandfathers and various railway uncles in Leharia, which he always called Zinderneuf. He had explained with shining eyes the sentimental possibilities of desert forts, marauding Bedouin, stolen jewels, and violent death. Now he was bright-eyed about chance meetings while whistles echoed.

"Second class passenger," Frankie said. "But I put her in first class because she is very beautiful."

"Yes," Shiv said. Actually she was rather plain, but Frankie was dedicated to romance.

Frankie ran his finger down a list on a board. "Mrs. Shanti Chauhan," he said.

"Fine," Shiv said, unaccountably irritated. He walked down the length of the platform, trying to find again his imperturbable velocity of a moment ago. At the end of the platform he waited, sitting on a green bench. He fanned himself with a folded *Times of India* and tried not to think. But as always the images skipped and skittered at the back of his head. He spread the newspaper across his knee but then was drowned by the vast turbulence of the world, its fires and refugees and ruined cities. A letter-writer called "Old Soldier" wrote, "Whether these men of the so-called Indian National Army were prompted by a version of patriotism, or gave in to fear of unspeakable persecutions by the Japanese, is scarcely to the point; that they took up arms against their former comrades is certain. They betrayed their vows to their units and their army and their king, and a soldier who is false to his *namak* can expect only two things: court-martial and the ultimate penalty." Shiv saw them falling, their bodies riddled and holed. He shuddered. So he shut his eyes and with a slow twist of fear in his stomach gave himself up to the uncertain currents of memory. Then Shiv's nostrils were full of Hari's smell, the slightly pungent aroma of life itself, cotton and perspiration and flesh, springing muscle, the same hair oil he used himself but sweeter on Hari. Now Shiv opened his eyes and his face was covered with sweat. There was a whistle, softened by distance.

He stood up and waited. He felt very small now, and under the huge sky he waited for the two events to come together, the busily grinding three-thirty from Lucknow and himself. He could see them moving closer to each other, the loco on its tracks, and his life, brought to each other in a series of spirals. He took a step forward and now it was a matter of another one to the edge. He could see the train, a black circle, huffing smoke and getting bigger. He began to think of calculations, of the time it would take to put one foot in front of another, of velocity and braking distance. He noted the red fragments from a broken *khullar* next to the tracks and determined that he would jump when the shadow of the train fell on them. That was close enough. The train came faster than he had thought it would, and now the sound enveloped him. He felt his legs twitch. He watched the red clay and then at the last moment turned his head to look down the platform. He saw in the swirl of colours a grey figure, motionless. He jerked his head back, felt the huge weight of the engine, its heat, and began his step forward, seeing the black curve of the metal above him, slashed in half by the slanting sun, the rivets through the iron, and then he staggered back, pulled himself back, an arm over his head.

Shiv found himself sitting on the ground, knees splayed outward. The bone at the base of his spine throbbed. He picked himself up and hurried past the first class compartments as the train screeched mournfully. She was stooping to pick up a small brown attaché, and he was sure she saw him coming. But she turned her face away, an expression of anger on her face, and walked resolutely towards the door of a carriage, where Frankie Furtado stood with his clipboard. She went past his smile with her eyes downcast, into the carriage, and afterwards sat in a compartment with half-lowered shades. Shiv stood outside, wondering at himself. He could see her arm. Twelve minutes passed, and then Frankie waved a green flag, leaning suavely to one side, and quite suddenly the train was gone. Leaving only a black wisp fading, and Shiv with his questions.

———

Frankie had an alphabetical list of names: "Madhosh Kumar, Magan Kumar, Nand Kumar, Narendra

Kumar . . ." He read from these every evening when Shiv visited him in his room behind the National Provision Store, in his desert lair, his lonely eyrie festooned with pictures of Ronald Colman. Frankie was the handsomest man Shiv had ever seen, with his gently wavy hair and his thin moustache and fair skin, and they were trying to find a screen name that would encompass and radiate all the mysterious glamour of his profile. Usually Shiv enjoyed the distraction of holding the name up to imaginary bright lights, of writing it into the magazines which Frankie collected and hoarded with incandescent seriousness. "Nitin Kumar Signs with MovieTone," or "Om Kumar Dazzles in Mega-buster" were all tried, tested and classified and estimated and measured, and found wanting in the analysis. This discussion took place always on the little *chabutra* in front of Frankie's room, with the spokes of Frankie's bicycle glinting in the moonlight. There were a few bedraggled bushes at the bottom of a brick wall, and a *chameli* tree overhanging the wall from Lala Manohar Lal's garden. The Lala's two daughters were of course in love with Frankie, but tonight even the sight of them hovering on the rooftop across the way like two bottom-heavy nightingales took nothing from Shiv's enormous yearning.

He was filled with a longing so bitter that he wanted all over again to die. He felt as if he was gone from himself. This was not the numb descent towards an inevitable stillness, no, not that at all. Now, in the darkness, Shiv felt a quickening in the night, a throb like a pulse that moved far away, and he was acutely aware of the smallness of the *chabutra* and how tiny Frankie's room was, with its one sagging *charpai* and the chipped white plaster on the walls and the crudely shaped green windows that could never completely close. Even the moonlight didn't hide the dirt, the dishevelled ugliness and cowpatties of a small *mofussil* town one step away from a village.

"Have you seen her before?" Shiv said. His voice was loud. He was angry, and he didn't know quite why.

"Yes," Frankie said. He stood up straight, alive with pleasure. "Twice before. She comes through

14

every two or three months, I think. Looking so beautiful and so alone."

"Going where?"

"I don't know. She catches a *tonga* outside the station. I think to the cantonment. Her attaché has stencilling on it."

Four miles from the station there was a brigade headquarters and, further away, an aerodrome.

"She's married," Shiv said. "Probably going to visit her army husband."

"Air force," Frankie said. "And why would she be visiting instead of staying in a lovely air force bungalow? And when she showed me her ticket I saw that she had others. Connections to all over the country, man. Why?"

"I don't know," Shiv snapped back. "I don't *know*. And why would it matter to you and me anyway? She's a married woman."

Frankie raised an eyebrow. He put a hand on his hip and his shoulder rose and fell in a long exaggerated shrug. Shiv saw that it was a gesture too large for life, impossible in its elegance, but in the silver

15

light it was entirely conceivable and exactly right, as if the world had suddenly changed, moved and become just a little larger, just enough to contain Frankie Furtado. Frankie, who swept his hair back now and turned majestically away, ridiculous and beautiful. Shiv shut his eyes, pressed on them until he felt pain.

Frankie sang: "*Kahan gaya ranchor? Duniya ke rahane valon bolo, chcheen ke dil mera, kahan gaya ranchor?*" His voice was good, light and yet full of intensity, and ample and rounded with its delight in its own skill. Shiv fled from it.

———

A cut on the palm of a right hand. Small, not too large, but ferocious in the straightness of its edges, in the geometry of its depth. Another on the left forearm, from the same straight edge. This is what Shiv remembered. As he walked home along a dusty lane he remembered the dark pearls of blood frozen on the pale skin. In the morgue he had found the cuts unbearable to look at, this damage, these rents in the surface and the lewd exposure of what lay underneath. Now he clung to the still shape as the only reality. It was the world stripped of all its fictions, this dead body on a grey stone slab, the smell. In only a minute or two, in a lane off Chandni Chowk, a whole life came to merely this, all of Hari's idealisms, his Congress membership and his Nehru-worship, his belief in change and the careful asceticism of his three khadi *kurtas* and his blushing appetite for mangoes, all of it gone to an odour of rot. All of it ready for the fire. Shiv held out an arm in the darkness and took careful steps with his fingertips on a wall. In the memory of the dead body of his brother there was a certain safety. There was a certain logic there, a brilliant lesson about the nature of the world. This Shiv knew. In Frankie's falsities, in his fantasies about the past and the future, there was certain disaster. To believe Frankie, to believe in him, that he could exist in Leharia, Shiv knew, was to risk an unfolding in his own chest, an expansion of emotion that would let in, once again, a certain hell of hope and remorse. He had left this behind.

"Did you have a good evening?" Shiv's brother-in-law, Rajan, liked to sit in an armchair in the courtyard of their house after dinner. Shiv could see the curve of his bald head, and the rounded shapes of his shoulders.

"Yes," Shiv said, and shut the door to his room behind him. He knew Anuradha *akka* would hurry out of her bedroom in a moment, and want to give him food. He was unspeakably rude, and they were used to this. They had patience. But Shiv lay on his bed and wrapped death around himself. He could hear a bird calling outside, solitary and plaintive. Shiv knew that finally the bird would stop crying out, his sister and her husband would stop whispering to each other and sleep, the house would settle into a late silence, a quietness that would echo the slow creaking of trees into his head. He would feel his self, his soul turn and turn inwards, again and again, until it was as thin-drawn as a wire, shiny and brittle. It was not a good feeling but he knew it well, and it was better than everything else. He waited.

———

He found that he was waiting for her. As he cycled around town, from one tuition to another, he anticipated each turn in the rutted lanes, even though on the other side of each corner there was always the same pool of stagnant water, the same goat leaving a trail of perfect black pellets, the same two familiar *dehati* citizens of Leharia with their flapping *pajamias* and "Ram-Ram, Shiv Bhaiyya." At the station, Shiv sat on platform number one and watched the trains. Frankie smiled fondly and hummed *Mere piya gaye Rangoon* under his breath every time he strolled by. Rajan believed that Shiv had at last and only naturally succumbed to the charm of steam, that he had become a lover of the black beauties that raced across the horizon, an aficionado of their hulking grace and their sonorous power. He came and sat beside Shiv often, in the quiet moments of the day. "Beyer Garrat loco, latest model, 1939. Used only on the express. Look at that! The total heating area, including the superheater, is more than four thousand square feet."

Shiv listened to the tales of the trains, and imagined the tracks arrowing across the enormous plains to the north, and to the south across the rocky plateau, and hairpin turns over vertiginous ridges, and through black deserts. He thought of her sitting by a half-closed window, her hands in her lap, and wondered what she was doing. Who was she? Where was she going? Why did she return? As the questions came he understood that everything had changed. Now, at night, instead of long wakefulness and empty, tiring slumber for an hour before dawn, he found a twisting, sweaty, dream-ridden sleep. He saw long visions of childhood, fantastic and drenched with blood, and also adventures in forests, and unspeakable seraglios in which *apsaras* with long black hair twisted against each other. He was hungry all the time, and ate his sister's *uttapam* with a relish that made her beam and write gladdened letters to his parents. And one evening in August he actually asked Frankie Furtado to sing *Kahan gaya ranchor*. Frankie tilted himself against the wall next to a window, a slim streak of white against the black, black clouds, turned his face to the light, and sang as the rain billowed over the green fields.

Shiv believed that he would know, somehow, when she came back, that he would sense her presence in the twisting lanes. Even as he laughed at the Frankie influence on his thoughts he believed this. But when she came he missed her entirely. He was unfastening the cycle-clips from his calves outside the station when Frankie came running out and found him.

"Where were you? She's here," Frankie said, clutching hard at Shiv's shoulder. "She's here."

"Where?" There was a solid sheet of water falling from the crenellated roof of the station, spattering loudly against the flowerpots below.

"On the 24 up. She had to wait quite a while for a *tonga*, all this rain, I suppose. Then finally she left ten, fifteen minutes ago."

21

Shiv threw his leg over his cycle and skidded out into the rain. His plastic cap tumbled away and splashed into the mud but Shiv rode on, spraying an arc over the road. He rode hard, leaning against the pedals, feeling the water pull at the wheels in the deep parts. The rain hit him violently in the face, coming straight and parallel to the road, and he laughed. His chest was drenched and cool, but under his raincoat he was sweating. He cycled through the main bazaar, where the little shops looked cosy under the darkness of the rain. Then he struggled against the long slope where the road opened out into the orderly rows of the Civil Lines and the cantonment, and the wind pushed against him, but then he saw the shape of the *tonga* ahead, sailing on the water. He pedalled madly, and then he came up on it and slowed. He could hear the muffled clip-clop, the swish of the wheels. There were small curtain-like pieces of cloth drawn around the back of the *tonga*, but he could see her feet on the backboard. Shiv went along now, not near but not too far. He listened to the rain, and the sound of his own breathing, in and out. He had no idea what to do next.

Shiv stopped at a big double gate. There was a wide curving drive leading up to the square white building Shiv knew was the military hospital. He could see, as he blinked his eyes against the sting of the drops, the *tonga* stopped next to a balustraded entranceway, the dripping horse, her attaché case, and her, as she hurried, head bent, through the doors. Shiv waited, cold now, shivering. Finally, when it was dark and he could only see the rows of lighted windows, glowing and unreadable, he turned and wheeled his cycle home, coughing.

He woke up the next morning with a fever. His sister saw it in his reddened eyes and careful walk, but he burst past her protestations and rode to the station. It was very quiet now, no rain, and the silence was wet and fresh and everywhere green, and he felt himself lost under the enormity of the smooth grey sky. Frankie was waiting for him at the entrance to the station.

"She's in the waiting room," Frankie said.

Shiv nodded impatiently. He walked down the length of the platform, past the fire buckets filled with sand and the two coolies wrapped in checked red sheets and a cloud of *bidi* smoke. Outside the waiting room, he stood for a moment, running hooked fingers through his tangled hair. His eyes burnt drily. He pushed the doors ajar and went in, keeping his gaze on the floor. He found the *matka*, and as he dipped into the water with the ladle he found that he was really thirsty. He poured into a glass, drank, and turned.

"Hello," he said.

She said nothing, and looked solemnly at him. He realized suddenly what it must take from her, how much courage and strength to travel the length and breadth of the country alone, in these times.

"My name is Shiv Subramaniam," he said. She looked down, and he was then ashamed of persecuting her as many others must have done on her travels, and he edged away toward the door. But Frankie was backing in, carrying a tray with a teapot and cups.

"Mrs. Chauhan," Frankie said, swooping down on the small table in front of her. "Tea for you." He laid out the cups with smart little movements. "There. Mr. Subramaniam, who is our esteemed Station Master *saab*'s brother-in-law, will serve." He looked at Shiv. "Please." Then he bowed to Mrs. Chauhan, and was gone.

For a moment Shiv stood absolutely still. He felt dizzy. Then he stepped up to the table, bent over, and picked up the teapot. He was angling awkwardly at the waist and the teapot felt very heavy, but he poured one cup, and then the other. He put the pot down.

"Sugar?" he said.

"No," she said. Her voice was oddly husky. She took the cup and the saucer and held it in her lap. Shiv stood stupidly still, and then realized she was waiting for him. Quickly he picked up his cup and saucer, and tried to keep it steady in his trembling hand. He took a sip, and it was very hot and he usually took sugar, lots of it, but he drank rapidly and watched her. Finally she raised her cup and drank.

"You've come here before," he said.

"I go to the hospital at the base," she said.

"Ah," he said. His legs were shaky, and very carefully he sat on the chair to her left. Looking at her directly, he saw that she was very thin, that the way she held her head alertly above her bony shoulders gave her a kind of intrepid dignity.

"I'm looking for my husband."

"Your husband?"

"He's missing in Burma," she said. "He is a pilot."

There was nothing to say to this.

"He is a fighter pilot," she said. "He was in the first batch of Indian fighter pilots in the RIAF. He was flying a Hurricane over Burma in 1942. They were protecting transports. They were attacked by Japanese fighters. The last his wingman saw of him was the plane losing height over the jungle. The plane was smoking. That was all they saw."

She was speaking in an even voice, and the sentences came steadily after one another, without any emotion. It was a story she had told before.

"So, at the hospital . . .?"

"I talk to the men who come back. Before it was only a few. Now they're all coming back. From the prison camps. And the others, from the INA." She looked at Shiv. "Somebody must have seen him, met him. Only today I met a soldier from the Fourth Gurkhas who said he had heard about a fighter pilot in a camp on the Irrawaddy."

She had complete confidence. The names of the units and of the faraway places came to her easily.

"So I'll go to the army headquarters in Delhi, find out who was in that camp. Talk to them."

She nodded. She finished her tea, and put the cup back on the tray. Then she folded her hands in her lap, and it seemed she was now content to wait, either for the train, or the man from the Fourth Gurkhas, or a flier in a plane above the trees. There was again that strange quietness, as if the world had paused. Again Shiv felt that he was vanishing into the huge wash of grey above, the sudden and endless green to the horizon. He shut his eyes.

"The man in the hospital told me he had seen the most evil man in the world."

Shiv opened his eyes. "Who? The Gurkha told you this?"

"No, no," she said impatiently. "The man in the next bed. He was from the Twenty-third Cavalry."

And then she told him the story of the most evil man in the world. Shiv listened, and the words came to him through the burning of his blood and the din of his pulse. The shadows drifted in the room and then she was finished. Then Frankie came in and said the train was near, and they walked down the platform, and Shiv held her attaché case in his right hand, and walked slowly behind her. They stood on the platform until the train came, and when the train pulled away neither she nor Shiv waved or raised a hand.

Frankie walked up to him. "You don't look very well," Frankie said.

Shiv fainted.

———

His sister was pressing a glass against his lips. Shiv choked on the hot milk and turned his head away from the bitter metal of the glass.

"You have to drink, Shiv," Anuradha said. "There is this weakness you have to defeat."

He raised himself up against the pillows, and his body felt light, ready to float. He drank the milk, and saw that Frankie was sitting at the far end of the darkened room. Shiv finished, and handed the empty glass to Anuradha, still feeling the hot liquid burble in his throat. After Anuradha left, Frankie opened the window a little, so that Shiv could see the swirling sky. And there were still the steady drops splattering on the stone outside.

"Crazy man," Frankie said. "But you'll be all right. Just a little flu you've got."

Shiv tilted his head, yes, and the room moved around him.

"She was talking to you for a long time," Frankie said, smiling. "I saw. Very seriously. What was she telling you?"

"She," Shiv said. He stopped for the friction in

his throat. He tried again. "She told me about the most evil man in the world."

Frankie turned, came and sat next to the bed. "What do you mean?"

Shiv didn't quite know. What she had told him, how she had told him, that day yesterday was now left to him only in fragments. He remembered it now only across the dark sea of sleep, lost behind the distant horizon of sunset and illness. He reached back and held only slivers. But there was something else in his throat, complete and whole. "I think this is what she told me." He cleared his throat. It hurt.

I touched my mother's feet and she sent me to war with an *aarti*. "Ja, beta," she said. And so I left her, and the smell of incense, and went. My grandfather and my father had served in the Twenty-third Cavalry, and there I went. Our colonel McNaughten said our job was to kill Germans, and we killed them. We are fighting evil, he said. In the mess there was a cartoon of

Hitler crushing Africa under his jackboots. So we killed them on Ruweisat Ridge, on the Rahman track, on the Aqaqir ridge. I saw huge stony fields and burning tanks and trucks and upended guns till the eye could see no more. Long black columns of smoke and oily burning at the root. We killed them. And they killed us. Mahipal Singh, Jagat Singh, Narain Singh. Kirpal Singh in the night when we ran into the First Life Guards and they shot us and we shot them.

On the Tel the Germans tried a counter-attack. They came at night down a narrowing slope, after a barrage with what they had left. Across a narrow wadi, facing the slope, the 1/9th Suffolk had dug in. They had machine gun positions and anti-tank and mortars sighted in on the slope. All night the Germans came and the Suffolk cut them down. They could hear the Germans calling to each other. Then the light of flares and the Suffolk firing. The Germans came and tried and tried again and then again. All night it went. Then in the

31

morning the Suffolk counterattacked, and then
they opened up and let us through, followed
by Bren gun carriers. I was driving the lead
armoured car, not only in the troop but in the
regiment. We came down the Suffolk side of
the wadi with the wheels and tracks crunching
on the rocks and we could see the bodies of
the Germans covering the slope opposite. They
had fallen so close, so many, that it was as if all
the rock were covered with faded olive cloth,
a green carpet. German bodies. Of course not
all of them were dead. But we had killed them.
We bounced into the bottom of the wadi and the
engine growled and we struggled against a lip of
rock and the heavy wheels bit into the ground
and rocks crumbled and sprayed and then we
were almost over and then I stopped.

I stopped the car, I brought it to a halt.
Through the driver's slit, through the armour
plate, not six feet away and ahead, a German
was looking at me. He was very young, propped
up on an elbow, that strange golden-white hair,

and he had the bluest eyes I had ever seen. He was looking at me. He had the bluest eyes I had ever seen, against the dust-covered face, eyes the colour of a sky you or I had never seen. I could not tell if he was dead or alive, and he was looking at me. "Damn it, Huknam," Captain Duff crackled into my ears. "Push on." But I could not tell if the man with the blue eyes was dead or alive, and he was looking at me. "Huknam, you're holding up the whole advance," Captain Duff shouted, and I thought of the troop behind me, and then the regiment, and the army and armies and all the countries beyond, all held up behind me. So I let in the clutch and the man with the blue eyes was looking at me for a few seconds more and then we went over him and up the slope and the regiment followed. The engine was thundering in my ears as we crunched up and up but as we went up I could not have heard it but I heard them, them outside on the ground calling out. "*Mutti*," they said. "*Mutti*." We came up over the ridge and they had nothing left, but thirty-four miles on and the next day we came into a line of anti-tank guns. They were very close to the ground and well-camouflaged and they caught us well, two other cars in our troop burning in the first minute. We saw the muzzle-flashes and tumbled one, but then there was a whang behind and above me and I was deaf, and I raised my hatch and jumped out. The sand was on fire and there was a burning behind my ears and on my shoulders. I fell down and got up and ran as I could and then I knew my shoulders were on fire. I rolled and rolled and finally it was out. The car exploded and I never saw any of them again, not Captain Duff or the others. It must have been an eighty-eight.

They put me in a field hospital and finally in Cairo they cut my left arm off. When I had jumped off the car I hadn't known but it had been shattered all to pieces. They cut my arm off and it was strange but I felt no pain, not then and not afterwards. But there was something else. When finally I could walk I went into the courtyard of the hospital, I liked to sit on the bench there. There were birds in the roof and in the rafters and they came down to be fed, and there was a fountain. One day I sat on the edge of the fountain, which was dry. But there was a Rajput who brought out a bowl of water for the birds and put it, the bowl, into the fountain. In this bowl of water I saw that my eyes had turned blue. I went inside and found a bathroom with a chipped mirror and still my eyes were blue. My eyes were blue and as I looked at the man, the man who was before me, I saw that his face was cruel and the eyes were blue and still, neither alive nor dead, strange in the brown face. He had the bluest eyes in the world. And this was how I met the most evil man in the world.

When Shiv finished he was exhausted. He lay back on the pillows and let his eyes shut. Yet he was afraid to sleep. He felt Frankie pull the sheet up and lay it over his chest.

"Did she see him?" Frankie whispered. "Did she see his eyes."

"Yes," Shiv said. "She saw him and she said he had the bluest eyes she had ever seen, not only for an Indian but for English or German or anything else."

After a moment, Frankie said, "Sleep."

Shiv stretched under the sheet, turned his neck against the pillow. He felt tired but better, achy but relaxed. He knew he would get better. He slept.

———

Shiv got so much better that his parents started talking about marriage. He splashed around town on his cycle, singing. He laughed at the yellow furrows that his wheels carved deep in the water. His sister and her husband were relieved and then a little concerned, made uneasy by the sudden change, but in Delhi his parents were convinced that all was now well and it was time for him to settle, everything should be settled. Meanwhile Frankie Furtado watched the trains eagerly, even the ones that were not going towards Bombay. He told Shiv that he would use a network of assistant station masters throughout the country to find her, to trace her movements and predict her return. But Shiv was confident that she would come back, and soon. He said to Frankie, "Not to worry, my friend. She'll come back." Frankie looked disappointed as his dream of a clandestine spy network vanished, but still, a month and three days later, it gave him tremendous satisfaction to discover her name on a list of advance reservations. He found Shiv on platform three, where he was sitting with his arms flung over the back of a bench, looking out at the slow wind swaying the tall grass.

"My friend," Frankie said. "Eleven hundred hours tomorrow."

"What?" Shiv said.

"Eleven hundred hours," Frankie said out of the side of his mouth, his hands in his pockets and looking away significantly.

Shiv looked up and down the empty length of the platform. "Yes, that, but what?" he said.

Frankie raised an eyebrow, and Shiv burst out laughing. "What, her?"

"Yes, yes, her," Frankie said, a tremendous smile on his face and not a spy any more.

Shiv got up, put his arm through Frankie's, and led him down the platform. "Frankie Furtado," Shiv said. "You're a madman."

Frankie flung his hair back, and raised a declamatory hand to the sky. "I have drunk of the chalice of wine," he said. "And I am mad." And Shiv thought that Frankie was indeed mad, and he was mad too, and if there was wine the world must have drunk it too.

The next day, though, Shiv was very rational, very cool when she stepped from the train. "Mrs. Chauhan," he said, and carried her attaché case to the *tonga*.

"What did she say?" Frankie said, pulling at Shiv's elbow as the *tonga* pulled away. "What did you say?"

"Nothing," Shiv said. Frankie was stricken. "Don't worry, Frankie. She'll come back and I'll tell her something."

"What?"

"I don't know. Wait and see."

The next day Shiv found her again in the waiting room. Again Frankie brought in a tray with cups and a teapot, and again Shiv poured. She drank the tea without speaking, as before, but afterwards she cleared her throat.

"Did you find anybody from the camp on the Irrawaddy?" Shiv said.

"Yes," she said. "But he wasn't in that camp. But there was some other news, of an escape at another place. So many of them are back."

Shiv nodded. They had come back in thousands, from the army, from the prison camps, and from the other army which had fought against its former comrades. And they had hope for her, each of them, and despair.

"But," she said. "But I met somebody, a woman."

"Yes?"

"At the bus station at Bareilly. She was a Congress-*walli*."

Shiv nodded. He started to say, my brother was also, but it caught in his throat. "Yes," he said.

"She told me something."

"Yes?"

"She told me about a woman who ran backwards into the future," she said.

Afterwards, when she, Mrs. Chauhan, had gone, gone away on the train without a wave or a backward glance, Frankie put an arm around Shiv's shoulder and walked him to the end of the platform. "So?" Frankie said. "So how did you get along?"

"Swimmingly," Shiv said.

"Tell me all. What did she tell you? Learn anything new?"

"Nothing about her, really."

"But you were in there so long. What, then?"

"Take a walk, Frankie?"

"Where? There? No, you must be crazy."

But Shiv could see that Frankie was dying to know, to be told, and so of course Frankie came along with Shiv, in spite of the green grass stains on his white pant legs, and they walked up the slope a far way. And Shiv told him what she had said.

Zingu heard a speech by a politician. Zingu had been coming home to his hut at the end of the day, and it was dark, and so Zingu stood in the dark behind a broken wall and listened to the politician. The politician stood under a petromax lamp and said that all men were equal. The townspeople applauded. Zingu went home in the dark, and he slept quietly, but in the morning he told his wife not to go to work. He told her that there was no need to carry shit any more. This is what they did, Zingu and his wife. They cleaned the latrines of the twice-born by hand and carried it away on their heads in baskets. But Zingu said his son would be a judge. He told his wife that all men were equal. His wife told him that he was crazy, and took her stinking basket and went to the village. But they killed Zingu anyway, and his son. He wandered around with his son saying all men were equal, and so they caught him in the open fields behind Dhiresa's mansion and cut Zingu and his son to pieces. One of them held up Zingu's foot at the end of a *talwar* and said, look at the size of this thing. All men aren't equal. And that was the end of Zingu, and his son.

But that's not the end of it. Because in Dhiresa's mansion, on the roof, his daughter-in-law Janamohini was drying her hair. In the winter sunlight Janamohini was lying on a *charpai* on the roof, her long, long black hair spread like a cloud, wet and curling and shining and dark. She was young and beautiful and loved, and the mother of two sons and one daughter, and through the delicious sunny sleep of the contented she heard far away the snick and whick of the swords as they cut Zingu. She stretched reluctantly out of her drowsy dreaming, feeling the welcome soreness in the muscles from the night before, sat up, and looked out over the parapet and saw Zingu's foot at the end of a sword. She covered her face and screamed, and many people came running up, uncles and aunts and cousins, and comforted her, and told her it was nothing. And then she was content, and smiling again, and she ate well that night.

But in the darkness, from the roof, she saw a glow. There were fires in the fields. She saw campfires in the fields, and figures dancing about them. She watched them, for a long time, and she could hear singing. She could hear music. Finally her husband called out to her from the courtyard below, and she went down the stairs. She was happy, she laughed and played with her children, yet later she slipped out of the house, by the small door inset into the spiked gate at the back of the house, and she went into the fields. Janamohini walked for a long time, guided by the glow shining off the sky, and finally she found her campfires. There was indeed music, and singing. There were people dancing near the fires. Janamohini saw they were of despised caste, that they were celebrating a wedding, that they were drinking liquor and eating meat, and the music was happy and they welcomed her, and so she danced with them. She drank their liquor and ate their meat. And she whirled around the campfires.

But then her husband and his brothers, who had found the open door, came and took her back to Dhiresa's mansion. Janamohini screamed and fought, but the husband said there had been no campfires, no dancers, no liquor, no meat. He said there had been nothing at all. Now Janamohini shrieked, my feet, my feet, look. She said her feet were pointing the wrong way. Upside down they are, she said. Look. And she began to walk backwards. They tried to stop her, but she walked backwards, faster and faster. She began to run backwards. Her husband wept, and she said, can't you see? If I go fast enough, back and back, I will leap into tomorrow. And her husband wept.

They tried many exorcists then, many a priest, two Tantrics, and a doctor from the town. But Janamohini always walked backwards after that, looking for tomorrow.

But that's not the end of it. Because on that night, no, the next morning, when the people in Dhiresa's mansion woke up, the aunts and uncles and cousins, they saw that Janamohini's hair was white. During that night, and that night only, all of her glorious hair, all of it long and luxurious and oiled and to her knees, all of it, turned white. From the scented clinging black of love it went to the white of madness. All in one night. All this happened in one night.

"And," Shiv said, "she, Mrs. Chauhan, that is, she said she asked the woman who told her this, is this true?"

"Yes," Frankie said. "And the woman said?"

"The woman said—yes, it's true, I tell you it's true, because Janamohini was my mother. I saw her hair turn white, she said, I saw it white in the first light of the morning. All of it white. And I am twenty-two and my hair is white. And perhaps my daughter's hair, if I have a daughter, will be white also."

"And it was white, her hair? The woman who told Mrs. Chauhan this?"

"White, yes. She was young but her hair was white as salt on a beach, as metal in the moonlight, as the sun on a flag."

"That's white," Frankie said. "Poor Zingu."

"Poor Zingu."

They walked back towards the long length of the station, with the huge mottled sky above, and the wind pulled at their shoulders.

"What about her, Shiv?" Frankie said. "Did you find out anything about her? The husband?"

Shiv thought, his head tilted back to the grey glory of the clouds. "I don't think so," he said.

"You didn't ask?"

"No."

"Don't you want to know, Shiv?"

Shiv shrugged. He knew he was smiling awkwardly. "I know it's strange," he said. "And I suppose I do want to know. And I suppose I'll find out. But right now, today, I just like her name."

"Shanti?"

"Yes."

Frankie put his hands in his pockets, hunched his shoulders, and laughed. "Some people fall in love with dark eyes. Others with pale hands glimpsed beside the Shalimar. Why not a name then?"

"It's a good name."

"I know," Frankie said, and put an arm around Shiv's shoulder. "But, brother, a fact now and then is a good thing."

"You're talking about facts, Frankie the lover?"

"Lovers are practical, my young friend."

"Really? That's interesting. It means, I think, that I'm not a lover."

Frankie nodded gravely. But as he looked away Shiv saw that he was smiling. The grass made a sighing sound as they walked.

Now Shanti—and this was how Shiv thought of her—came to Leharia often. As the trial of Dhillon and Sahgal and Shah Nawaz was argued in Delhi, and lawyers and advocates and judges jousted with each other to establish once and for all who was traitor, who was hero, she followed anecdotes and hints and the visions of delirious men up and down the country. Now she pursued the merest whisper, a shadow seen on a jungled hillside years before, a fevered groan floating across fetid bunks laden with dying men. But each time she came she told Shiv of something that she had heard on the way, the things that came to her on all the ways that she went, some incident, some episode, told to her by an old man, a young bride, a favourite son, an angry daughter-in-law, a mother, an orphan, and all of it true, true, and true. She told him about The Ten Year Old Boy Who Joined the Theatre Company of Death, The Woman Who Traded in Oil and Bought a Flying Racehorse, The Farmer Who Went to America and Fell Through a Hole to the Other Side of the World, The Moneylender Who Saw the True Face of the Creator, Ghurabat and Her Lover the Assassin Who Wept, The Birth of the Holiest Nun in the World and The Downfall of the Mughal Empire. And each time Shiv said, it's true. Of course it's true.

But one day in January she had nothing to tell. Or perhaps she hadn't the strength to speak. She sat in her usual chair, an empty teacup in her lap, and her eyes fluttered shut as Shiv watched. He saw the way her mouth trembled and the slump of her shoulders from the taut line he had come to know. He took the cup from her and put it on the table, and with the tiny rattle she opened her eyes.

"They let them go," she said. "They went home."

"Who?"

"Dhillon, Shah Nawaz, and Sahgal."

The papers had exulted in huge black letters: "GUILTY, BUT FREE!" They had gone home, the three, heroes or traitors, finished with it one way or the other. They had been convicted, cashiered, but finally they were told, you're free, you can go. They would go home, and even if nothing was finished, not ever, they would batten away the memories and find new beginnings. All of them were going, going home. Shiv thought of them, the thousands and thousands of them, jostling and jolting across the country in trains, in buses and bullock carts. He pulled a chair toward Shanti, set it squarely in front of her. He sat down in front of her, his hands in his lap. At the back of his neck there was a trembling, as the words pulsed in his chest, exerting a steady pressure against his heart: you're free, you can go.

"I heard something," Shiv said.

"What?"

He cleared his throat, and for a moment he felt fear, blank and overpowering, and he was afraid of speaking, he felt profusion pressing up against the clean prison he had built for himself, but then he looked into Shanti's eyes and he spoke. He told her what he had heard. Afterwards they sat in silence, and Shiv was grateful, because his shoulders ached and he was very tired.

When she was in her compartment, settled in the window, Frankie came strolling down the platform to announce that the train was delayed for twelve minutes. Shanti nodded, but Shiv was too lost in a sudden panic of emotion to say anything. He felt terror and joy mixing in his stomach, and a slow creep of pleasure at the sunlight across his shoulders, and grief. Frankie looked at him, and then took him by the arm and led him away.

"This time you were talking," Frankie said. "And talking and talking. About what?"

"I was telling her something."

"*You* told her a story?"

"Yes."

"Tell me."

Shiv tried. He opened his mouth, and tried to form the words, but they were gone from him. "I can't," he said, trembling. He gestured at his throat, meaning to explain the tumult under the skin.

"All right, sure," Frankie said, baffled but quick to the chase. "I'll ask *her*."

And he did. Frankie stood by the window, his head cocked to one side. Under the long flutter and hiss of steam, Shiv could hear her words.

Amma woke in the morning and cleaned the house. She cleaned the storerooms, the rooms around the courtyard, she swept the dark mud

51

floors and wiped the mantlepieces and the
tops of the doorways. She put new wicks in the
lanterns and filled them with oil. She washed
the red brick of the courtyard and emptied out
the ashes from the *choola*. And the children
going in and out of the house, through the
big door with iron hoops, told their mothers,
Amma's cleaning. And the women of the village
said, one of her children is coming.

It was a small house, with a granary at the
rear and a good well. Amma's grandfather
had built it in some time so far away that she
thought of it as beyond numbers. He had built it
solid and strong, and she came back to it after
her school-teacher husband died of typhoid.
She came back with four children, two sons and
two daughters, the oldest just eleven, to this
village called Chandapur, and here she lived
and grew old. Her name was Amita but the
village called her Amma. She could not read or
write, but she educated her children. There was
money, just so much, from the farming of her

land, and she lived quietly and with a simplicity that was exactly the same as poverty, but she sent her children to school in the city. In her house books were sacred. She wrapped them in red cloth and stacked them on a bed in the biggest of the rooms in her house. Amma lived in a village and ate only twice a day but her children went to boarding school. Her eldest son went to Roorkee and became an engineer. Amma went sometimes to the cities, north, south, east, and west, to visit her children, but came back always to her house in the village, fiercely alone and happy.

It was this engineer son who came home that day. He sat on a *charpai* in the courtyard and spoke to the men from the *panchayat*, who came and sat around him in a circle and smoked. There were women in the kitchen, helping Amma and laughing with her. She had a wicked tongue, and liked to talk. They could hear her laughing in the courtyard, as they listened to the engineer. There were children running in and out of the house. The engineer was telling them, everyone, about the end of the war. He was wearing a white shirt, dark blue pants, and his hair came up on his forehead in a wonderful swell which the villagers, knowing too little, couldn't recognize as stylish. He had a high querulous voice, and he was telling them about the American bombs.

"The bomb killed a city," he said. "There were two bombs. Each finished a city." He snapped his fingers, high in the air. They looked at him, not saying a word, and he felt the stubborn peasant scepticism gathering around his ankles, that unmovable slow stupidity. He was irritated, rankled now as he used to be when his mother laughed at his modernisms. *Aji-haan*, she would say, unanswerable. It baffled him that his most sophisticated explanations of cause and effect were defeated easily by snorting homespun scepticism, sure-yes, *aji-haan*. He could see her now, standing in the sooty doorway to the kitchen, her arm up on the wall, listening. "Fire," he said. "Whoosh. One moment of fire and a whole city gone."

"How?" It was Amma. Her hair was white, and she was wearing white, and she had a strong nose and direct eyes. The engineer looked up at her, a glass of milk in his left hand. "If you break a speck," he said. He didn't know how to translate "atom". "You release energy. Fire." Amma said, "How?" Now the children were quiet. Amma took two steps forward. "How?" The engineer gestured into the air. "It's like that thing in the *Mahabharata*," he said finally. "That weapon that Ashwatthaman hurled at Arjun." "The Brahmasira?" Amma said. "That was stopped." "Not this one," the engineer said, turning his hand palm down. "They used it." Then the food was ready and he ate.

Nobody noticed until the next morning that Amma had stopped talking. "What happened?" the engineer asked. "Why aren't you talking?" A little later he asked, "Are you angry with me? Did I do something?" Amma shook her head but said nothing. She refused to talk to her friends, and to their children. Now some people thought she had taken a vow of silence, like Gandhi-ji, and others thought that she had been witchcrafted by some secret hater. The engineer was annoyed, and then concerned. He wanted to take her to the city, to a doctor. She put a hand on the ground and shook her head. But she wouldn't talk, couldn't. Finally he left, her son. In the weeks after her other children came, one by one, and still she spoke to nobody. She smiled, she went about her daily business, but her silence was complete and eternal.

First it was just one child, Nainavati's daughter, eight years old. Her skin cracked on her hands. Her mother rubbed her skin with *neem*-leaf oil, and held her close. The next morning the cracks were open, a little wider, and spreading to the elbows. And that afternoon Narain Singh's son had it too. There was no bleeding, no pain, only the lurch of Nainavati's heart when she looked at her daughter's hand

and saw the white of bone at the wrist. A
week later all the children in the village were
splintered from head to toe. Looking at each
other they wept with fear, and their parents
were afraid to hold them. Pattadevi said it first.
One morning her baby, ten months old, gurgled
against her thigh, and Pattadevi raised her
head, forgetful and so smiling, and she saw the
pulsating beat of a tiny heart. Pattadevi shut her
eyes tight, and in her anguish she said, "Amma's
son brought it home, with his Japanese bomb."
That was then the understanding of the village,
true and agreed upon.

Finally the horror was that they grew used to
it. The months passed and they were shunned
by the neighbouring settlements, and certainly
they did not want to go anywhere. Life had to
go on, and so they tended the crops, saw to the
animals, built and repaired, and lived in a sort
of bleak satisfaction, an expectation of precisely
nothing. On the three hundred and sixtieth day
Amma came to the *panchayat*.

They were sitting at their usual places under the *pipal* tree, the old men, and the powerful, and then the others. They fell silent when Amma walked among them, surprised by her appearance in an assembly of men, and a little afraid of her, her witchy quiet and her confident walk. She sat under the *pipal* tree. In her hand she had a letter.

"What is that, Amma?" the *sarpanch* said. "A letter from your son? What does he write?" He took the letter from her, as he usually did, tore it open, and began to read. "Respected mother . . ."

"I want to praise," Amma said.

"What?" the *sarpanch* said, dropping the letter.

"The kindness of postmen, their long walks in the summer sun, their aching feet. The mysterious and generous knowledge of all those who cook, their intimate and vast power over us. The unsung courage of young brides, their sacrifices beyond all others, their patience.

The age of trees, the years of their lives and their companionship. The sleeping ferocity of dogs—I saw two kill another last week—and their stretching muscles, their complete and deep and good happiness with a full stomach and a long sleep."

The *sarpanch* opened and closed his mouth. Before long all the women gathered too, with their children, and the whole village listened to Amma.

"The long song of those who drive trucks on the perpetual roads. The black faces of the diggers of coal, and their wives who try ever not to hear the sound of rushing water under their feet. The staggering smell of the birds that clean bones, their drunken walk with its anxious greed. The roofs of the village houses in the morning, seen from the *ghats* above the river, and the white glimmer of the temple above the trees. The roaring familiarity of the dusty brickmakers with fire. The painful faith of unrequited lovers."

The villagers listened to her. One of the children noticed it first. He tugged at his mother's hand, but she was rapt. He held her index finger and pulled it to and fro, and the gold bangles on her wrist jingled, and she looked down. He held up his arm to her, and she saw the cracks were gone. Then others saw it too. No one could see it happening, not one fissure or the other closing, but if they looked and looked away and looked back, they could see the skin becoming whole. And Amma was talking. She praised the sky, the earth, and every woman in the village, and each of the men, even the ones known for sloth, or cruelty. Then they brought her food, and water, and she talked.

When she finished talking the next day the children were well. Much later, the *sarpanch*, who was sitting on a *charpai* in her courtyard, said to her, "Well, Amma, your son brought the sickness, and you fixed it."

"What did you say?" Amma said, and for a moment the *sarpanch* was afraid that for all his dignity she would throw the teacup she was holding at his head. "My son brought it?"

"You have to admit that he came, and then they were sick."

But Amma rolled her eyes. "*Aji-haan*," she said, and that was that.

By the time Shanti had finished telling the story, the train was an extra two minutes late, and Rajan came out of his office and looked angrily down the platform. Frankie waved his flag and the bogie began to move. Shiv walked beside the window, and he watched the shadows from the bars move across Shanti's face. With every step he had to walk a little faster.

"Will you marry me?" he said.

"What?"

"Will you marry me?"

A shudder passed over Shanti's cheeks, a twist of emotion like a wave, and she turned her face to the side in pain, as if he had hit her. But then she looked up at him, and he could see that her eyes were full. He was running now.

"Yes," she said.

He raised a hand to the window as she leaned forward, but the train was away, and the platform came suddenly to an end. Shiv stood poised at the drop, one hand raised.

"Is it true?" It was Frankie, eager and open-faced. "Is it true?"

"What?"

"Your story, you stupid man, is it true?"

"Of course it is," Shiv said, waving his arm in front of Frankie's face. "It is. Look."

Frankie was looking past the arm with a deductive frown. "What happened to you? Why are you grinning like that?"

"She's going to marry me."

"She is? She? You mean you asked?"

"And she said yes."

"But where is she going now?"

"I don't know."

Frankie raised his arms in the air, clutched at his hair, threw down his red flag and green flag and stomped on them. "God help this country, with lovers like you," he said finally. Then he took Shiv by the arm, and took him home, to Frankie's lair, and began to plan.

————

Two months and three days later, in a train to Bombay, Shanti slept with her head on Shiv's knee. They were in an unreserved third class compartment, and Shiv was thinking about the four hundred and twenty-two rupees in his wallet. Next to the notes he had a folded yellow slip of paper with the address of one Benedicto Fernandes, who was Frankie's first cousin and an old Bombay hand. In the sleeping dimness of the compartment Shiv could see the nodding heads and swaying shoulders of his fellow travellers, two salesmen on their way back from their territories, a farmer with his feet propped up on a huge cloth bundle, his wife, a muscular mechanic, and others. They had made space on the one berth for the newlyweds.

They had been married in a civil ceremony in Delhi. This after Shiv had written to his father, "My Dear Papa," and "I must ask your blessing in a momentous decision," and had received a curt reply telling him to come home, and containing no blessing, or word of affection. He had written again, and this time received two pages of fury, "disobedience" and "disgrace to the family" and "that woman, whoever or whatever she may be". Meanwhile Anuradha was tremulous, and Rajan had muttered about what one owed to one's parents, and what a bad influence that Furtado fellow was. But finally Frankie had saved them. He had found Shanti, her letters and Shiv's had gone to his address, and he had made the arrangements, set up their rendezvous, lent money, and had gone with Shiv to wait for the night bus at the crossroads.

"What if they do something, Frankie? What if you lose your job?"

"All to the good, my friend. I shall be free." In the moonlight Frankie threw his head back. They stood arm in arm, with fields and bunds stretching away on all sides. Frankie was humming something, a song that faded gently under the chittering of the crickets. When the headlights appeared to the east, appeared and disappeared, Shiv said, "Thanks, *yaar*."

"*Yaars* don't say thanks," Frankie said. Then the bus roared up to them, heavingly full of passengers, and luggage, and a half dozen goats. Frankie found a place for Shiv's suitcase on the roof, and a space for him to squat in the doorwell. Shiv hugged him, hard, and Frankie held him close.

"Go," Frankie said.

"Frankie, come to Bombay," Shiv said as the bus pulled away. Frankie raised a hand, and that was the last Shiv saw of him, in a silvery swirl of dust and a fading light.

Now Shiv looked down at the head on his knee, at the rich thickness of the dark hair. It occurred to him that they hadn't kissed yet. After they had signed the register they had both paused, and then Shiv had thanked the registrar. Then they had gone to the station, awkward in the *tonga*, each keeping to one side of the cracked leather seat. Shiv had seen kisses in the movies, but he hadn't ever kissed anyone. He looked around the compartment, and then, with the very tips of his fingers, he touched Shanti's cheek. It was very soft, and he was overcome by a knowledge of complete unfamiliarity, of wonderment, and complete tenderness. "Shanti," he whispered under his breath. "Shanti." How strange it was, how unknown. How unknowable.

Shiv's fingers moved over her cheekbone, and now she stirred. He watched her come awake, the small stirrings. Then she tried to stretch, and found the hardness of his hip, and the end of the berth, and woke up. He could see memory coming back, shiverings of happiness and loss. She sat up, rubbed her face. He smiled.

"Do you have a photo of yourself?" she said.

"What?"

"A photo. Of yourself."

"You woke up thinking about this?"

"I went to sleep thinking I don't have one."

Shiv leaned back, raised his hip with a curl

of pain through his back, and found his wallet. Under the four hundred and twenty-two rupees and behind Frankie's cousin's address he found a creased snapshot.

"Here," he said. "Actually it's Hari. But it doesn't matter. We're identical."

She was looking down at the photo, smoothing away the ridges. "No, you're not."

"Yes, we are."

"No, really, you look different. Very different. See?"

He looked, and there was the well-known twist of the torso, the smile. He knew exactly and well the leaves behind the hair, the tree, and the garden.

"Maybe," he said. "Maybe."

"It is," she said, certain. "You are." She took the photo from him and opened her purse, found a small black diary and put the picture away.

"How about one of yourself?" he said.

She hesitated, then opened the diary to the back. In the picture she gave him she was laughing, leaning towards the lens. But in front of her, there was a smiling man, very handsome, dark hair and keen pilot's eyes, and her hand rested on the epaulettes of his jacket.

"You're different, too," Shiv said.

"I was younger, yes," Shanti said.

"More beautiful now, I meant," Shiv said, and she smiled at him, and he wanted very much to kiss her but the compartment was stirring now. They sat back and away from each other as the travellers awakened themselves with thunderous yawns. Shiv put the photo in his shirt pocket, and raised the shutter on the window. He leaned into the fresh wash of air, the glad early grey of the land. You are changed, Shiv thought, and I am, and we are all something new now. And then he looked up, and saw the red sun on a ridge, and he was filled with excitement and foreboding. The mountains here were unfamiliar to him, different in their age, their ridges, and the shape of their rivers.

"We must be near Bombay," he said.

One of the salesmen leaned over to the window, scratched at an armpit, looked about with the certainty of a professional traveller, and shook his head. "No, not quite," he said. "Not yet, *beta*."

Shiv laughed. He looked at Shanti. She was laughing with him. "We'll get there," he said.

———

Now there was night outside. In the dark I wiped at my face, and listened to the clear clink of ice in Subramaniam's glass. There was something I wanted to say, but it seemed impossible to speak. Then I heard a key turning in the door.

"That must be my wife," he said, and got up. "She and her friends have a Ladies' Tea on Sundays. Where they drink anything but tea." A light came on in the corridor.

"Are you sitting in the dark?" she called, and another light flickered, a lamp just inside the room. She had the same white hair as him, and round gold-rimmed glasses, and she was wearing a dark red sari.

"This is young Ranjit Sharma," Subramaniam said. "From the bar, you remember."

"*Namaste, namaste*, Ranjit," she said in answer to me. "Sit, sit. And you, you've been giving him those horrible chips? Has he been eating them, Ranjit? And drinking? He's not supposed to, you know. And did you go to Dr. Mehdi's for the medicine?"

He hadn't, and so she shooed him out, and I made her a drink. She drank Scotch and water and talked about horses. Also about a long vacation that they were to take, and their reservations.

"You're feeling better, then?" I said.

"Me? Me? Oh, I see. You mustn't believe a word he says, you know." She took off her glasses. Her eyes were a lovely flecked brown in the lamplight. He had said nothing about her eyes. "The medicine is for him, not for me."

"Is it serious?"

"Yes."

"I'm sorry."

She shrugged, just like him, and I thought they looked exactly like each other, transformed by the years together, and I tried to smile.

"Don't be sad," she said. "We've had our life, our Bombay life. Come on, you'll stay for dinner. But you'll cut onions before."

————

It is night, and I am walking in my city. After dinner, Subramaniam came down to the road with me, and walked a little way. What happened to Frankie, I asked. Did he come to Bombay and become a movie star? For a long moment Subramaniam said nothing, and we walked together. No, he said, no, to tell you the truth, Frankie died. He was killed. Those were bad times. But there was somebody else who came to Mumbai and became a movie star. When I come back from vacation, he said, I'll tell you that one. You had better, I said. At the *naka* he shook my hand. Goodbye, chief, I said.

I am walking in my city. The island sleeps, and I can feel the jostling of its dreams. I know they are out there, Mahalaxmi, Mazagaon, Umerkhadi, Pydhuni, and the grand melodrama of Marine

Drive. I have music in my head, the jingle of those old names, Wadala, Matunga, Koliwada, Sakinaka, and as I cross the causeway I can hear the steady, eternal beat of the sea, and I am filled with a terrible longing. I know I am walking to Bandra, and I know I am looking for Ayesha. I will stand before her building, and when it is morning I will call up to her. I might ask her to go for a walk, I might ask her to marry me. If we search together, I think, we may find in Andheri, in Colaba, in Bhuleshwar, perhaps not heaven, or its opposite, but only life itself.